SELTZER

UP FROM

A HANDY GUIDE TO 4 JEWISH GENERATIONS
BY PETER HOCHSTEIN • DRAWINGS BY SANDY HOFFMAN

WORKMAN PUBLISHING , NEW YORK

LIBRARY OF CONGRESS CATALOGING IN PUBLICATION DATA
HOCHSTEIN, PETER.
UP FROM SELTZER.

1. JEWS—UNITED STATES—CULTURAL ASSIMILATION—
CARICATURES AND CARTOONS. 2. UNITED STATES—SOCIAL
CONDITIONS—CARICATURES AND CARTOONS. I. HOFFMAN,
SANDY. II. TITLE.
PN6231.J5H57   741.5'973   80-54617
ISBN 0-89480-145-7 (PBK.)   AACR2

COVER AND BOOK DESIGN: SANDY HOFFMAN

WORKMAN PUBLISHING COMPANY, INC.
1 WEST 39 STREET
NEW YORK, NEW YORK 10018

MANUFACTURED IN THE UNITED STATES OF AMERICA

FIRST PRINTING MARCH 1981

10   9   8   7   6   5   4   3   2   1

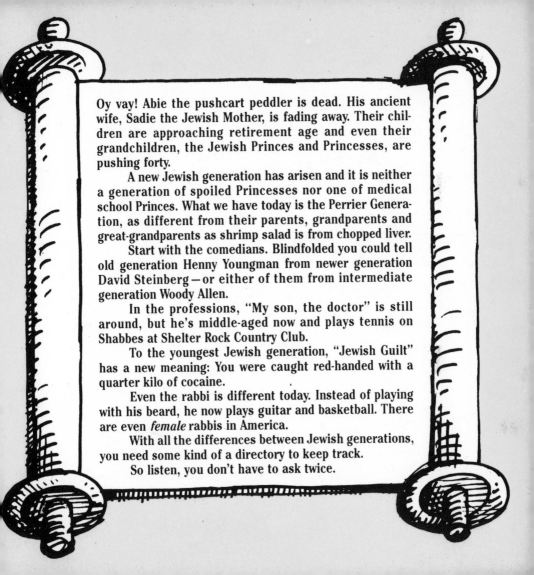

Oy vay! Abie the pushcart peddler is dead. His ancient wife, Sadie the Jewish Mother, is fading away. Their children are approaching retirement age and even their grandchildren, the Jewish Princes and Princesses, are pushing forty.

A new Jewish generation has arisen and it is neither a generation of spoiled Princesses nor one of medical school Princes. What we have today is the Perrier Generation, as different from their parents, grandparents and great-grandparents as shrimp salad is from chopped liver.

Start with the comedians. Blindfolded you could tell old generation Henny Youngman from newer generation David Steinberg—or either of them from intermediate generation Woody Allen.

In the professions, "My son, the doctor" is still around, but he's middle-aged now and plays tennis on Shabbes at Shelter Rock Country Club.

To the youngest Jewish generation, "Jewish Guilt" has a new meaning: You were caught red-handed with a quarter kilo of cocaine.

Even the rabbi is different today. Instead of playing with his beard, he now plays guitar and basketball. There are even *female* rabbis in America.

With all the differences between Jewish generations, you need some kind of a directory to keep track.

So listen, you don't have to ask twice.

THE NAME OF THAT NICE JEWISH BOY

1ST GENERATION	**2**ND GENERATION	**3**RD GENERATION	**4**TH GENERATION
Yussel Pincus	Irving Pincus	Robert Pincus	Sean Pincus

THE NAME OF THAT NICE JEWISH GIRL

Yetta Koplowitz	Shirley Koplowitz	Barbara Koplowitz	Kimberly Koplowitz

JEWISH BEVERAGE OF CHOICE

1ST GENERATION:
Seltzer water ("Fer 2 cents plain").

2ND GENERATION:
Scotch, bourbon or rye.

3RD GENERATION:
Pouilly-Fuissé, well chilled.

4TH GENERATION:
Perrier water (Fer 2 dollars, fancy).

TYPICAL JEWISH MALE OCCUPATION

1ST GENERATION:
Sells on the street from a pushcart.

2ND GENERATION: Owns a
retail store or a dress factory.

3RD GENERATION:
"My son, the doctor."

4TH GENERATION:
Leads sensitivity
training sessions.

TYPICAL JEWISH FEMALE OCCUPATION

1ST GENERATION: Worked in a sweatshop until marriage, then became a housewife.

2ND GENERATION: Became a housewife the day she was born.

3RD GENERATION: Taught school until she got married.

4TH GENERATION: "My daughter, the doctor."

IF YOUR SON IS SMART HE'S...

1ST GENERATION:
"A regular Einstein."

2ND GENERATION:
"A regular genius."

3RD GENERATION:
"A gifted child."

4TH GENERATION:
"Maladjusted."

ORIGIN OF THE PASSOVER WINE

1ST GENERATION: Grandpa Yussel made it in the cellar.

2ND GENERATION: Manischewitz made it in Brooklyn.

3RD GENERATION: "It's a Chateau Figeac, but I hired a rabbi to bless it for the holiday."

4TH GENERATION: "After I optioned the Napa Valley vineyard, I had them put this aside for the holiday."

FEMALE SEXUAL ANXIETY COMPLEX

1ST GENERATION:
"The Cossacks are coming!"

2ND GENERATION: "My son is spending too much time with that shiksa."

3RD GENERATION: "Suppose I get hit by a bus and when they get me to the hospital, they discover my underwear is manufacturers' seconds?"

4TH GENERATION: "But will he still want to be my lover ten years from now, when I'm fifty and he's twenty-nine?"

MALE SEXUAL ANXIETY COMPLEX

1ST GENERATION: "What if I *never* earn enough to get married?"

2ND GENERATION: "What if she gets pregnant and we *have* to get married?"

3RD GENERATION: "What if she gives me a case of clap?"

4TH GENERATION: "What if she comes on to me?"

MY VISIT TO THE DOCTOR

1ST GENERATION: "When I learned what the operation costs, I said forget it—I'd rather live with the pain."

2ND GENERATION: "Listen darling, I wouldn't make you nervous by telling you why I need an operation. All you have to know is, it begins with the letter *C* and it's probably fatal."

3RD GENERATION: "He said I could go on the Scarsdale diet, increase my polyunsaturates and exercise to reduce my triglycerides—or if I don't like doing all that, cut out the chocolate cake."

4TH GENERATION: "A nip here, a tuck there, and for only $10,000 you'll look twenty years younger."

THANK YOU LETTERS
FOR BAR MITZVAH PRESENTS

1ST GENERATION: *Dear Uncle Herschel, Thank you for the beautiful fountain pen. I'm saving it for when I become an accountant.*

2ND GENERATION: *Dear Uncle Murray, Thank you for the $50 savings bond. I'm saving it to help pay for college.*

3RD GENERATION: *Dear Uncle Steve, Thank you for the $500 check. I should have written to you six years ago, but I wanted to wait until I could tell you how I used the money. The building on the other side of this postcard is the Eiffel Tower.*

4TH GENERATION: *Dear Cousin Kevin, Oh, wow! A sterling silver nose spoon!*

PORTNOY'S COMPLAINT

1ST GENERATION: "Every time I touch her, she gets pregnant. With four children, my life is over."

2ND GENERATION: "Whenever I touch her, she says she has a headache."

3RD GENERATION: "I can forget sex tonight—she just had her hair done."

4TH GENERATION: "Kimberly says it would be meaningless for us to make love while she's having an extramarital relationship with Bryan."

MRS. PORTNOY'S COMPLAINT

1ST GENERATION: "Sol looks so tired, don't know what to do. He's killing himself with work."

2ND GENERATION: "How can I run this house on $75 a week?"

3RD GENERATION: "What do you mean we can't afford a Mercedes? Do you want the neighbors to think we're on welfare?"

4TH GENERATION: "I can forget sex tonight. Lance just had his hair done."

JEWISH FEMALE'S FASHION PHILOSOPHY

1ST GENERATION: "So who needs to buy? I'll sit down at the sewing machine and in half an hour, I'll make."

2ND GENERATION: "On Sunday, you'll go to Irving's factory and he'll sell it to you wholesale."

3RD GENERATION: "No thanks, Mom, I want my *own* mink coat."

4TH GENERATION: "Where's Ralph Lauren's signature?"

JEWISH MALE'S FASHION PHILOSOPHY

1ST GENERATION: "It belonged to Yussel, but now that he's dead, just shorten the pants and it'll fit you perfect."

2ND GENERATION: "Dress British, think Yiddish."

3RD GENERATION: "If you wear a necktie, how will anybody see your gold chains?"

4TH GENERATION: "Where's Ralph Lauren's signature?"

HOW TO TELL
A DEEPLY RELIGIOUS MAN

1ST GENERATION: Never misses morning prayers, evening prayers, Shabbes or High Holiday services.

2ND GENERATION: Never misses Shabbes or High Holiday services.

3RD GENERATION: Usually makes it to High Holiday services.

4TH GENERATION: Never misses going to Acapulco on Yom Kippur.

WHERE THAT NICE JEWISH COUPLE LIVES

1ST GENERATION: A hovel on the Lower East Side: $68 a month.

2ND GENERATION: A nice little house in Levittown: $5,000 down, plus $200 a month for 20 years.

3RD GENERATION: A condo high-rise in Beverly Hills: $100,000 down, plus $3,000 a month forever.

4TH GENERATION: An all-organic commune in Vermont: $290 for the tepee, plus 20 food stamps a month.

WHERE GRANDMA LIVES

1ST GENERATION: "After Yussel died, she moved in with us. It's crowded, but what can you do?"

2ND GENERATION: "She says that since she has nothing more to live for, she wants to die in the same apartment where she spent her whole life with Max."

3RD GENERATION: "She bought an apartment on Fifth Avenue with the life insurance money, but she still spends winters in Miami Beach."

4TH GENERATION: "I'm not sure. If this is April, she might be in Palm Springs with her lover."

JEWISH EXERCISE

1ST GENERATION: Rocking on the porch, fanning yourself, complaining about the heat.

2ND GENERATION: Going for a nice long walk in the country, then taking a swim.

3RD GENERATION: Tennis lessons.

4TH GENERATION: Nude skydiving.

BIG JEWISH BREAKFAST

1ST GENERATION:

Bagel and lox
with a glass of tea.

2ND GENERATION:

Bagel and lox
with a cup of coffee.

3RD GENERATION:

Bagel and Nova Scotia salmon
with a cup of espresso.

4TH GENERATION:

Two croissants, an omelette aux fines
herbes and a glass of skim milk.

JEWISH ANSWER TO THE POLITE GREETING, "HOW ARE YOU FEELING?"

1ST GENERATION:
"So how *should* I be feeling?"

2ND GENERATION:
"Don't ask!"

3RD GENERATION: "You really want to know? My head aches, I have cramps, I was vomiting all night, my blood pressure is up, and I'm a nervous wreck. And furthermore..."

4TH GENERATION:
"Mellow, man. Mellow."

JEWISH MARRIAGE DISASTERS

1ST GENERATION:
Never got married.

2ND GENERATION:
Married a gentile.

3RD GENERATION:
Married a black.

4TH GENERATION:
Married somebody of the same sex.

ORTHODOX JEWISH HEADWEAR

1ST GENERATION:

2ND GENERATION:

3RD GENERATION:

4TH GENERATION:

A JEWISH KID'S ALLOWANCE

1ST GENERATION: 5 percent of whatever he makes peddling newspapers on the street.

2ND GENERATION: 25 cents a week.

3RD GENERATION: $2 a week.

4TH GENERATION: His own credit cards.

JEWISH DIETARY RESTRICTIONS

1ST GENERATION: Anything that isn't kosher.

2ND GENERATION: Anything that isn't kosher except Chinese food.

3RD GENERATION: Anything with cholesterol.

4TH GENERATION: Anything with meat in it and anything that wasn't organically grown.

JEWISH FEMALE'S MARRIAGE ASPIRATIONS

1ST GENERATION: Hopes to marry an accountant (but settles for a pattern cutter).

2ND GENERATION: Hopes to marry a doctor (but settles for an accountant).

3RD GENERATION: Hopes to marry an oppressed black jazz musician (but settles for a doctor).

4TH GENERATION: Hopes to stay single and have a career (but settles for an oppressed black accountant).

JEWISH MALE'S MARRIAGE ASPIRATIONS

1ST GENERATION: Hopes to marry the fat daughter of a ribbon merchant (but settles for the skinny daughter of an impoverished rabbi).

2ND GENERATION: Hopes to marry the *zaftig* daughter of a wealthy garment manufacturer (but settles for the flat-chested daughter of a ribbon merchant).

3RD GENERATION: Hopes to marry a willowy shiksa (but settles for the fat daughter of a wealthy garment manufacturer).

4TH GENERATION: Actually marries a willowy shiksa (but she divorces him).

WHY YOU SHOULD CLIMB DOWN FROM THAT TREE, YOUNG MAN

1ST GENERATION: "If you get killed, it will serve you right."

2ND GENERATION: "If you get killed, don't come running to me."

3RD GENERATION: "A broken arm we can always fix, but what if you injure your mind?"

4TH GENERATION: "The karma up there is very bad, Jason!"

RITUAL EQUIPMENT
FOR CELEBRATING CHANUKAH

1ST GENERATION:

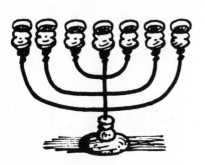

2ND GENERATION:

3RD GENERATION:

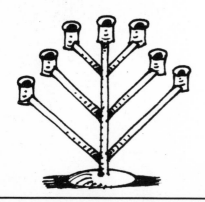

4TH GENERATION:

WHAT I MADE AT CAMP

1ST GENERATION: "Ten dollars in tips. Here Ma, buy yourself something nice."

2ND GENERATION: "A wampum belt, for you, Ma."

3RD GENERATION: "A wampum belt, for me, Ma."

4TH GENERATION: "A shiksa."

JEWISH DEFINITION OF A MILLIONAIRE

1ST GENERATION:
Once made $25,000 in one year.

2ND GENERATION:
Has $25,000 in the bank.

3RD GENERATION:
Has a million dollars.

4TH GENERATION:
Owes a million dollars.

CURE FOR NERVOUS TENSION

1ST GENERATION:
Work, work!

2ND GENERATION:
A drive in the country.

3RD GENERATION:
Valium.

4TH GENERATION:
Rebirthing.

CAUSE OF JEWISH WEIGHT PROBLEMS

1ST GENERATION: "What can you expect—she eats like a bird."

2ND GENERATION: "What can you expect—she eats like a bird."

3RD GENERATION: "What can you expect—she eats like a horse."

4TH GENERATION: "What can you expect—she eats like a horse."

JEWISH LEISURE UNIFORM

1ST GENERATION: "So who has time for leisure?"

2ND GENERATION: For her, a mink jacket over checked slacks. For him, a Hawaiian shirt over blue serge suit pants.

3RD GENERATION: Anything with an alligator on it.

4TH GENERATION: Unisex jogging suits with Pierre Cardin initials and Adidas running shoes. Sweatbands optional.

HOW TO ORDER LOX
AT THE APPETIZER STORE

1ST GENERATION: "So Hymie, take your thumb off the scale and weigh me a quarter pound lox. But not the *dreck* you sold me last week. Thief! It would hurt you to let me have that extra little sliver?"

2ND GENERATION: "A sixteenth of a pound of lox, Hymie, and slice it *thin* for a change."

3RD GENERATION: "Don't bother slicing the Nova Scotia, Hymie. It's going right into the food processor. We're making *saumon mousse.*"

4TH GENERATION: "Wait a second — is this fish organically grown?"

THE TRAGIC STORY OF MY CHILDHOOD PET

1ST GENERATION: "She was a wonderful cow, but when Grandpa Yussel lost his job, we had to eat her."

2ND GENERATION: "We were so poor, we couldn't afford a pet. I used to put a leash on my brother and teach him to pee on fire hydrants."

3RD GENERATION: "I had to give up my pet puppy dog when I was sixteen, because my mother was too sick to walk him for me."

4TH GENERATION: "We decided it was ecologically unsound to keep a boa constrictor in the city."

BIZARRE SEXUAL PROCLIVITIES

1ST GENERATION:
Likes thin women.

2ND GENERATION: Looks at ancient French postcards of men in tuxedos embracing women in chemises.

3RD GENERATION:
Makes love with the bathroom light on.

4TH GENERATION: Throws hot tub parties with bisexual couples and a horse.

FOUR WAYS TO PUNISH A JEWISH CHILD

ZETZ

FRASK

SCHMEISS

KNIP

THE OFFICIAL CAUSE OF DEATH

1ST GENERATION: "He worked himself to death so you could have a better life."

2ND GENERATION: "When he heard you flunked out of medical school, he died of a broken heart."

3RD GENERATION: "I *warned* him not to play tennis after a big lunch."

4TH GENERATION: "He blissed out on quaaludes."

JEWISH NECK CHAINS

1ST GENERATION:

2ND GENERATION:

3RD GENERATION:

4TH GENERATION:

DEFINITION OF A JEWISH WHORE

1ST GENERATION:
Flirted wantonly before marriage.

2ND GENERATION: Had sex before marriage with the man she married.

3RD GENERATION:
Slept around before marriage.

4TH GENERATION:
$100 a throw.

TYPICAL JEWISH VACATION

1ST GENERATION:
A bungalow in the Borscht Belt.

2ND GENERATION:
A resort hotel in the Borscht Belt.

3RD GENERATION:
Deluxe hotels in Europe.

4TH GENERATION:
A bungalow at Club Med.

EXCERPTS FROM A SUICIDE NOTE

1ST GENERATION: *My wife Yetta is dead. My sons Irving and Max have taken over my business and are running it into the ground. The grandchildren never visit. I have nothing left to live for. Somebody say Kaddish for me, if it isn't too much trouble.*

2ND GENERATION: *The business is bankrupt, my son the doctor is too important to return telephone calls, and my wife Shirley puts on perfume at night and says she's going to the movies. I hope you all have a wonderful time at my funeral.*

3RD GENERATION: *A cross-eyed woman is suing me for malpractice during wrinkle surgery. My wife is having an affair with the tennis pro. My children never write from the commune in California. Enjoy your lives, because I just rewrote my will leaving everything to the United Jewish Appeal.*

4TH GENERATION: *I have decided to reunite my karma with the universal wholeness of the ecosphere. Please scatter my ashes so that they won't intrude on anybody's space.*

A GOOD PLACE TO START A BUSINESS

1ST GENERATION: "Right downstairs. If we sleep over the store, we can even wake up and sell herring in the middle of the night."

2ND GENERATION: "Downtown. You couldn't find a better location."

3RD GENERATION: "In the suburbs. Who wants to commute?"

4TH GENERATION: "In Hawaii. I can write off the air fare and hold meetings in the swimming pool."

JEWISH EDUCATIONAL ACHIEVEMENT

1ST GENERATION: "I went to the 'School of Hard Knocks'—but my son will go to college."

2ND GENERATION: "I went to City College—but my son will go to an Ivy League school."

3RD GENERATION: "I went to Princeton and then Yale Medical School—but I believe in a less structured education for my son."

4TH GENERATION: "I go to Bennington—but I plan to get a Harvard MBA with my lady."

1ST GENERATION: "You ask what is the meaning of life? So I ask you, what *should* be the meaning of life? When you've got an answer to that, you'll know what life means."

2ND GENERATION: "The Scriptures tell us that life is a wonderful opportunity for people who otherwise wouldn't have had one."

HE INSCRUTABLE RABBI

3RD GENERATION: "You say you'll make a donation to Israel next week? I say donate now. Because remember: When the dike breaks, fingers are of no use."

4TH GENERATION: *"Hare Krishna, Hare Krishna, Rama Yana, Hare Krishna.* Have you ever stopped to wonder what these words mean to Jewish youth? You haven't, but Sun Myung Moon probably has."

MILESTONES IN JEWISH MEDICINE

1ST GENERATION:
Discovers chicken soup.

2ND GENERATION: Discovers that aspirin cures everything chicken soup can't fix.

3RD GENERATION: Discovers that psychiatry cures diseases that never existed before.

4TH GENERATION: Discovers that Rolfing and Scarsdale diets make disease unnecessary.

HOW TO TELL YOUR HUSBAND
YOU WISH HE EARNED MORE MONEY

1ST GENERATION: "So you work twenty-four hours a day! Lots of men work twenty-four hours a day. It would hurt you to work one extra hour?"

2ND GENERATION: "See these hands that you used to say were so beautiful? Wait until you see how they look after I start taking in laundry!"

3RD GENERATION: "Don't worry, Jeff. If I sleep with my boss just once, he'll give me a raise. *Then* you'll have more time to write poetry."

4TH GENERATION: "I'm moving out until you get your act together."

WHAT TO SAY IF YOU RECEIVE A GIFT

1ST GENERATION: "Take it back! What does an old lady like me need a wristwatch for anyway? I don't even expect to live another twenty-four hours."

2ND GENERATION: "It's very nice, but I won't wear it. Wristwatches always break on me. I'll put it in the vault, and when I die it can be a part of your inheritance."

3RD GENERATION: "I was hoping for a Longines."

4TH GENERATION: "Oh wow, thanks! I can get 50 bucks for this at a hockshop!"

JEWISH HOME FURNISHING GUIDE

1ST GENERATION:
1. Mezuzah
2. Floor lamp
3. Photos of parents in old country
4. Sewing machine
5. Kitchen table covered with oilcloth
6. Used rug on floor
7. Armchair protected by doilies
8. Window shades on windows
9. *Jewish Daily Forward,* Yiddish Edition
10. Radio plays only Yiddish-language station and static

2ND GENERATION:

1. Foot-long mezuzah
2. Wall-to-wall carpeting protected by plastic mat
3. Porcelain table lamp
4. Photos of grandchildren
5. Couch covered with plastic for protection
6. Armchair protected by plastic
7. Magnavox radio-TV-record-changer console, with plastic dustcover
8. *New York Post*
9. Dinette table covered by plastic tablecloth
10. Corpse accidently smothered in plastic

3RD GENERATION:
1. Sign in place of mezuzah: WE GAVE TO THE UJA
2. Danish mobile lamp
3. Own wedding photos
4. Cable TV
5. Glass coffee table
6. Bloomingdale's contemporary couch
7. Eames chair
8. Wall-to-wall carpeting protected by $10,000 oriental rug
9. *New York Times* and *Wall Street Journal*
10. Every best-selling book for the last ten years

4TH GENERATION:
1. Latin sign in place of mezuzah "If you don't swing, don't ring"
2. Parquet floor painted black to resemble asphalt
3. Industrial lamps
4. Signed Diane Arbus photos
5. Home computer set on "Tennis Doubles"
6. Table made from butcher block
7. Couch made from plastic bus seats
8. Laboratory-beaker drinking glasses
9. Armchair made of plumbing fixtures and pipes
10, 11, 12, 13, Stereo earphones for guests

JEWISH INTOXICATION

1ST GENERATION: "Oy! That mountain air is so fresh, when you breathe deep it makes your head spin."

2ND GENERATION: "Well, it's a special occasion, so have *two* shots."

3RD GENERATION: "Finish off the Mersault, and then I've got a Chateau Beychevelle breathing for the meat course."

4TH GENERATION: "Reverend Moon has given me a spiritual high."

HOW SHE KNOWS
HER HUSBAND IS CHEATING

1ST GENERATION: "After he came back from what he said was a long walk, I found a blond hair on his overcoat."

2ND GENERATION: "After he came back from what he said was a business trip, I found lipstick on his shirt collar."

3RD GENERATION: "After he came back from what he said was working late in the office, he couldn't get it up."

4TH GENERATION: "After he came back from what he said was jogging, I found strawberry jam in his jockstrap."

REACTION TO NEWSPAPER HEADLINE: "MAD SNIPER KILLS 10!"

HOW TO FIND JEWISH LITERATURE

1ST GENERATION: Go to the synagogue and read the Talmud.

2ND GENERATION: Go to the lending library and borrow Herman Wouk.

3RD GENERATION: Go to your bookstore and buy Philip Roth.

4TH GENERATION: You just did.

ENGLISH-YIDDISH

Great-grandpa Yussel and Great-grandma Yetta came to America speaking Yiddish. Their conversation was as subtle and precise as you'd expect from a language that had 432 ways to express feelings of pain.

However, the subtlety and precision didn't come from vocabulary alone. Inflection and grammatical construction gave varied definitions to words that would seem, to an outsider, to have only one meaning.

Remember, Yiddish flowered in the ghettos of Eastern Europe, where spies and Czarist agents—real and imagined—secretly lurked to denounce a poor Jew for heresy or subversion. To stay out of trouble, Jews learned to communicate through indirection, innuendo and subtle shadings of meaning. The consequence is that while Yiddish is extremely precise, it doesn't always mean what it seems to be saying.

Yiddish speech inculcates a state of mind, adaptable to the vocabulary of any language. Applying English vocabulary to Yiddish thinking creates an entirely new language called English-Yiddish.

English-Yiddish may *sound* like ordinary English with a funny inflection. But beware. What you hear may not mean what you think. You don't understand? Then study the conversation that follows.

TRANSLATION: Hello (familiar form).

TRANSLATION: How are you?

TRANSLATION: I am fine, thank you.

TRANSLATION: How is business?

TRANSLATION: Mind your own business.

TRANSLATION: What's all the scandalous talk I hear about your ugly daughter?

TRANSLATION: As you have obviously heard, a terrible thing has happened. My daughter has married a gentile.

TRANSLATION: Had your daughter been more patient, she might have found a more suitable mate.

TRANSLATION: I may be down but I'm not out, so get off my daughter's case.

TRANSLATION: Hold on, I'm not finished enjoying your misery over your daughter.

TRANSLATION: Just for that, I'm bringing up the subject of your mortally-ill wife.

TRANSLATION: Ah-hah! You thought I'd lie and say she's fine, but I've just made you feel horribly guilty by admitting the bitter truth!

TRANSLATION: You louse! Now I feel so guilty, I won't be able to sleep!

TRANSLATION: Your misery is accepted in lieu of an apology.

TRANSLATION: I still consider myself one up on you and won't let you forget it.

TRANSLATION: It's a pleasure sparring with you. We ought to do this more often.

TRANSLATION: I welcome these verbal altercations too, provided you first humiliate yourself by coming to *me*.

TRANSLATION: I bid you farewell by expressing concern for your gullibility and intelligence.

It's always a pleasure talking to you.

TRANSLATION: It's always a pleasure talking to you because I love a good fight.

ENGLISH-YIDDISH GRAMMAR

If the preceding conversation left you a bit puzzled, it may be because you don't understand English-Yiddish grammar.

There are parts of speech in English-Yiddish that simply don't exist in English-English. There are entire grammatical forms that would leave English-English grammarians scratching their heads in puzzlement. Here are some of the most important:

THE MORAL SUBJUNCTIVE ASSERTIVE SUPERIORATIVE

A subjunctive form of speech that positions the speaker as superior in social, financial or moral position to the listener.

This form works by stating a moral to an anecdote, which is then wished upon the listener—but not in the hope that the listener will actually achieve it. The object is to let the listener know he has *not* achieved it.

Example: "…and so my son, the doctor, is making half a million dollars a year—*you* should only do so well!"

THE SUBJUNCTIVE MISERATIVE AMBIGUATIVE

A subjunctive form that asserts terrible misery while giving the listener absolutely no clue about the cause of the misery.

Example: "What did the doctor say was wrong? You should only know!"

THE IMPERATIVE NEGATIVE MISERATIVE

Another form of speech that asserts misery, in this case by ordering the listener to cease an interrogation.

Example: "What's wrong? Don't ask!"

Note: In polite conversation, the hearer of an imperative negative miserative must immediately respond with, "So who's asking?" to which the only polite answer is, "So all right, I'll tell you!" (assertive capitulative).

THE VACUUMATIVE CONNECTIVE

In English, a connective is used in the *middle* of a sentence to connect two thoughts ("I felt ill, *so* I went home"). In English-Yiddish connectives have another purpose; they connect the *front* of a thought to silence. This proves the law of Jewish physics that conversation always seeks a vacuum.

Example: "So what's new?"

Note: There are only two vacuumative connectives in English-Yiddish. They are "so," and "nu?" "Nu?" is the more economical form, since it can be simultaneously a vacuumative connective and an open-ended question, the meaning of which is clear only to the listener.

THE PREPOSITIONAL DECLARATIVE NEGATIVE

For particularly emphatic declarations, most especially declarations of distaste, a sentence should always begin with a preposition and end with a negative declarative phrase.

Example: "With friends like him, I don't need enemies!"

THE OBJECTIVE ADVANCETIVE

Another way to give special emphasis to a declaration is to advance the direct object of a verb to the head of a sentence.

Example: "Trouble I could live without."

THE VACUUMATIVE CONNECTIVE INTERROGATIVE-ACCUSATIVE

THE INTERROGATIVE RESPONDATIVE SUBJUNCTIVE

Yet another subjunctive form of speech, in which a question (often attached to a vacuumative connective) is used as a response to a previous question.

Example: "So what *should* be new?"

THE CAPITULATIVE MANIPULATIVE

An elaborate rhetorical form in which the speaker pretends to capitulate to the wishes of the listener, while actually attacking with a cudgel of guilt that forces the listener to change his or her own position. The advantage of the capitulative manipulative is that it leaves the user blameless should his or her prevailing wishes lead to disaster.

Example: After ten years of scrimping and saving, you finally have enough money for a down payment on a modest house. You take a drive with your mother and tell her the news.

Your mother says, "Don't buy a house yet. Give the money to your Cousin Manny the Stockbroker. He'll double it for you in a month and you can buy a nicer house. Besides, we owe my sister Ethel, Manny's mother, a favor—and Ethel says Manny needs the commissions."

So far, you have *not* run into the capitulative manipulative.

What you have heard is merely a genetic imperative. However, you are being set up to have a capitulative manipulative unleashed against you when you resist your mother's advice, which you do next:

"Listen, Ma, Manny's a flake and a thief, and I happen to like the house I'm going to buy."

Now comes the capitulative manipulative. Your mother says, "Well, *if that's what you want,* who am I to hinder you? Just stop the car when we get to the middle of this bridge. I want to jump into the river—because I'll never be able to face my sister Ethel again."

Clobbered by guilt, you finally agree to purchase some stock recommended by Manny. Continuing in the capitulative manipulative voice, your mother says, "Well, *if that's what you want,* Ethel will be so happy."

Exactly one month later, your stock certificates are worth two cents on the dollar, trading has been halted by the SEC, and Manny has been indicted for securities fraud.

When you break the news to your mother, she will reply in the post-passive manipulative auto-absolutive interrogative:

"So why are you telling me? *You* were the one who wanted to buy stock from Manny. Did I force you?"

THE ABBREVIATIVE HORRIBILATIVE

Words that inspire terror are never written and rarely spoken, except in abbreviated form. At the head of the list is the name of the

Creator, which in English-Yiddish is always spelled "G-d." Names of awesome or terrifying diseases are similarly abbreviated.

Example: "Oy! You know what the doctor says he has? *C*!"

Obscenities must also be abbreviated. The author once heard a Princess schoolteacher complain of one of her kindergarten students: "Do you know what that terrible little boy said? He said *F*!"

How can you be certain what all the abbreviations mean? You have to live with them for at least twenty years. Otherwise, don't ask!